Party Time!

Mia's older sister

has been to *two* parties

at the fairy shop.

Now it's Mia's turn . . .

MORE NIBBLES TO SINK YOUR TEETH INTO!

BAD BUSTER
Sophie Laguna
Illustrated by Leigh Hobbs

COMING IN FALL 2006

THE LITTLEST PIRATE
Sherryl Clark
Illustrated by Tom Jellett

THE MAGIC WAND
Ursula Dubosarsky
Illustrated by Mitch Vane

Party Time!

Join Mia in the mystery and magic
of the fairy shop!

Janeen Brian
Illustrated by Beth Norling

RUNNING PRESS
KIDS
PHILADELPHIA·LONDON

9   8   7   6   5   4   3   2   1
Digit on the right indicates the number of this printing

Library of Congress Control Number: 2005928813

ISBN-13: 978-0-7624-2627-0
ISBN-10: 0-7624-2627-6

Original design by Melissa Frasier, Penguin Design Studio.
Additional design for this edition by Frances J. Soo Ping Chow

Typography: Fontesque, MetaPlus, and New Century School Book

This book may be ordered by mail from the publisher.
Please include $2.50 for postage and handling.
But try your bookstore first!

This edition published by Running Press Kids, an imprint of
Running Press Book Publishers
125 South Twenty-second Street
Philadelphia, Pennsylvania 19103-4399

Visit us on the web!
www.runningpress.com

Ages 6–9
Grades 1–3

To dear Barb
who loves a laugh.
Thanks also to the children at
St. Mary Magdalene's,
Elizabeth Grove.
J.B.

To Alice,
"Queen of the Palace."
B.N.

Chapter One

My name's Mia. I have a
big sister, Alice. She's been
to *two* birthday parties
at the fairy shop. She's a
lucky-duck.

"A fairy comes out of a
special room," Alice told

me. "It's only a lady dressed up. But she's got a beautiful pink cloak and wings. And a crown."

"Is she nice?"

"Of course she is,

Mia," said Alice a bit crossly.

"*Then* what?" I asked.

"She reads us a story
from a great big book. It's
about this fairy princess
who gets lost in the woods.
And it gets dark. But all the
animals save her."

"All the animals?" I
squeaked. "Even tigers and
lions?"

"It's a story, Mia!" Alice
looked even crosser. I

shifted closer to her on
the sofa.

"*Then* what, Alice?" I
said, softly.

Alice leaned back and put
her hands behind her head.
"We do a play about a fairy
princess," she said.

"*Then* what?"

"We dress up. And dance
around the maypole."

"Wow!" I cried and
clapped my hands. "What's

a maypole, Alice?"

"A big pole, with colored
ribbons hanging down. It's
so good," said Alice, and she
made her eyes roll. "Then

we get some gold dust and make a wish. And we have fairy bread and lemonade. And then we go home."

"That's *so* good," I sighed. I made a wish there and then. But I didn't have any special gold dust, so I knew it wouldn't come true.

Chapter Two

But guess what? It did!

I couldn't wait. I was going
to Emily's birthday. And
she was having her party at
the fairy shop!

"I'm going to the fairy
shop! I'm going to the fairy

shop! I'm going to the fairy

shop!" I sang.

Alice gave me another cross

look. "Be quiet, Mia," she said.

"I've already been there. *First*."

The shop was full of fairy stuff. Wings and wands and dresses. Everything looked sparkly and magic.

A lady with a big smile and big bottom took us into the storytelling room. We sat down on the floor.

There were drawings of dragons and elves and pixies and fairies all over the walls. There was hardly any room left for the light

10

switch! There was music too, special fairy music, coming from a black tape-recorder that you could hardly see, because it was behind The Wishing Tree.

I sat next to Emily and gave her a big grin.

"A fairy comes out soon," I told her.

"I know, Mia," said Emily, smoothing her dress over her knees.

Suddenly the music changed. I looked up. A fairy walked in from another room. She was smiling and waving her wand. She looked gorgeous.

I whispered to Emily,

"It's only a lady dressed up."

"I know," said Emily.

But the fairy wasn't

dressed up in pink.

She was dressed in blue.

"She's not the same Fairy
Queen," I said to Emily.
"She's not the same Fairy
Queen that Alice had."

"I don't care," said Emily.

"Hello, everyone!" said the
Blue Fairy as she sat down
on a big, flat toadstool.
"I'm the Blue Fairy Queen
and I'm going to tell you
a story."

"Is it about a princess who gets lost in the woods?" I cried. It might be the same story Alice told me about.

"No," said the Blue Fairy. She reached into a silver book-box. "It's another story."

"Oh," I said. "My sister has been here before. She said the fairy princess story was a good one, because all

the animals save her. Even
tigers and lions!"

"Hey!" cried Melanie.

"I think I know that story.

Mia, is it the one where the fairy princess is looking for her gold ring and . . .?"

"Yes!" I cried. "That's it! And it gets dark and . . ."

"Quiet!" The Blue Fairy put her wand straight up in the air.

"No talking!

I mean . . . Let's look at
this story, shall we? It's
about a dear little prince."

It was a boring story.
And the Blue Fairy kept
losing her place. She read
us one part twice. When
we giggled, she held up her
wand again.

Chapter Three

"Now we'll do a play," said the Blue Fairy.

"Let Emily be the princess," I said. "It's her birthday."

"Of course," said the Blue Fairy. Only she wasn't

smiling when she said it.

But then Ben started to sob. He was only four. *He* wanted to be the princess.

It wasn't the same.

We had to sing, "Princess Ben, Princess Ben, we've come to play with you."

And then he was supposed to say, "What will we play? What will we play?" Only he didn't because his skirt kept slipping, so I said it for him. Then he got cross and said it again. And everyone said it sounded stupid after saying it four times.

And the Blue Fairy
said it sounded even *more*
exciting. But it didn't.

So then Ben said, "Let's
play dragons!" And he
roared at Melanie.

Melanie laughed. "You're
a *princess*, not a dragon!"
His eyes sparkled.
"I'm a dragon princess."

"What do *we* do, Ben?"
I said. "Do you want
us to skip around
The Wishing Tree?"

"Yes!" he cried. "And I'll chase you! *Roar*!"

So we skipped fast.

Melanie tripped over the tape-recorder cord.

She said it didn't hurt.

But the music stopped, and the Blue Fairy had to kneel down and find the plug again.

"Emily should have a turn now," I said afterwards.

So the Blue Fairy got the skirt and crown from Ben and we did the play again. Only it was hard to hear because of Ben's sobbing.

"You can't be the princess twice, Ben," I said.

"Be quiet, Mia," said
Emily. "He's *my* cousin. *You*
can't say that to him."

"Okay," I said. Then I
turned to the Blue Fairy. "We
get dressed up now, don't we?"

Chapter Four

Emily put on the best pink
wings and a gold crown.
The wings had sparkling
patterns all over them.
She kept looking over her
shoulder so she could see
them. Then she waggled

her elbows to see if the wings flapped. When they did, she came over to watch the rest of us.

We put on silver crowns and white wings from the dress-up box. We got a wand too. Then we all tried to dong each other on the head with the wand! It was so funny.

"Stop!" The Blue Fairy held up her wand. "Wands up!" she cried.

We all held up our
wands. I looked at Emily.
"She's bossy!" I whispered.
"Fairies aren't supposed to
be bossy."

The Blue Fairy looked hard at me. "There'll be no maypole till we're all quiet little fairies," she said. It was then I noticed that her crown had slipped. It was sitting over one ear.

"Excuse me," I said.

"Do you need to go to the toilet?" she said.

"No."

Emily and the rest giggled.

"I just wanted to tell
you that your crown might
fall off."

That set everybody
laughing. Ben giggled and

started jumping up and
down.

He called out, "Crown, fall
down! Crown, fall down!"

The Blue Fairy stood
up very tall and straight,
with her wand in the air.

"WHO WANTS TO DO
THE MAYPOLE?" she said
quite loudly.

We all stopped laughing
and jumping.

Chapter Five

The Blue Fairy shouldn't
have joined in the maypole
dance. She was too big.
She muddled everyone up.

First she gave us each a
ribbon. Then she said, "All
right, little fairies—and

Ben fairy—we're going to have fun dancing round the maypole. Some of you go one way and some of you go the other—and make your ribbons go over and under, over and under. That's it. Round and round."

But then she joined in. And she went *under and over*, not over and under. And our ribbons got twisted and Ben got stuck in the middle.

"I'm all tied up!" he wailed.

So we untied him and he went over to The Wishing Tree to look at the lights. Then someone called out, "Let's get Emily!"

"No!" squealed Emily, laughing.

So we all grabbed a ribbon and ran round and round her, till Ben started to cry again. He thought Emily had disappeared.

The Blue Fairy had told
us that's what little fairies
do when they don't want
to be seen.

The Blue Fairy waggled
her arms. "Untie the girl!"
she cried. "Er, I mean, that's
it ... There, now we can see
her pretty face again."

She patted Ben and gave
him the gold box to hold.
Inside the gold box was
the wishing dust.

The Blue Fairy put some
wishing dust into our
hands. "What are you going
to wish for?" I asked Emily.

"I'm not saying," she said.

"I won't tell," I promised.

"No whispering secrets,"

said the Blue Fairy.

She was sitting back on the
big toadstool again.
"Otherwise your wishes
won't come true."

Just then, I saw her
lipstick was smudged.
But I didn't say anything.
We held the wishing

dust in our hands and
waited until the music
came on again.

"Close your eyes, fairies,"
said the Blue Fairy. "Now
make a wish."

I thought of a really good
one. But I couldn't tell.
Then we tossed the wishing
dust over our shoulder.

Only mine hit the Blue
Fairy. Right between
the eyes.

I bit my lip. "Will my
wish still work?" I asked.

"It *might*," said the Blue
Fairy. Only she had that
odd look on her face again.

I *really* wanted to tell her
about her lipstick. It looked
worse.

"Now let's have fairy
bread and lemonade," said
the Blue Fairy. She handed
round a tray.

Chapter Six

The fairy lemonade was
pink. "I think it's pink food
coloring," I said.

"I think you'll find it's pink
magic," said the Blue Fairy.
She was getting Melanie
a glass of water. Melanie

wasn't allowed lemonade.

"Hey!" I cried. "Look. Ben's got black bits in his fairy bread." I could see them between the sprinkles. Emily and I peered closer. "They're ants!" I screeched.

"Wahhh!" went Ben.

Everyone went, "Ants! I don't want any more fairy bread!"

"Yuk!" cried Melanie.

"Yuketty-yuk!" said Emily
and threw her bread into
the silver book-box.

"I hate ants!" cried Ben
and scrambled onto the big
toadstool.

"They're not *ants*!" said the Blue Fairy, but her eyes were real wide. 'They're little . . . they're little magic . . ."

"Are they little *special fairy ants*?" I said, trying to help.

"Well . . ."

"Ones that won't bite or sting or make you puff up or . . ."

"Yes, yes!" she cried. "That's right." Then she clapped her hands. "So we'll

say goodbye to them,
because I've got some
candy bags here. Who'd like
a fairy candy bag to take
home?"

"Me! Me! Me!" we all cried.

"Emily first," I said.

"Of course," sighed the
Blue Fairy Queen.

"Thanks, Blue Fairy,"
I said when I got my candy
bag. Then, seeing I was up
close, I said, "I thought

you'd like to know. Your
lipstick's smudged up near
your nose."

"Yes. Well, thank you for

telling me," she said. Only she didn't smile much. "Now goodbye, everyone. Goodbye, little fairies!"

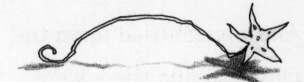

Chapter Seven

"What was it like?" said Alice, when I got home. Then she yawned. "Not that I really care, seeing I've been to the fairy shop before. *Twice.*"

"It was great, Alice!" I said.

"Just great! We donged
each other with our wands.
And Ben got tied up in the
maypole, and there were

ants in the fairy bread.
Everyone shouted,
'Ants! Ants! Ants!' It was
so funny."

Alice looked at me.
"Yeah?" she said. And her
voice went quiet. "You're
such a lucky-duck, Mia,"
she sighed. "Nothing like
that happened when I
went there."

I opened my candy bag
and looked inside. "Oh

well," I said. "Maybe if you get the *Blue* Fairy next time, it will!" I put a frog candy in my mouth.

Alice looked at me and smiled. "Yeah, that'd be good," she said.

"Do you want a candy, then?"

"Yeah, okay," said Alice, and looked inside the bag.

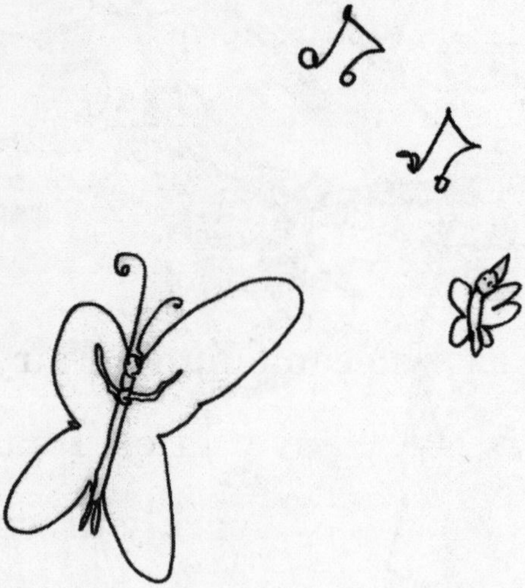

From Janeen Brian

When I was young, I spent time
making beautiful homes and
gardens for fairies. When I was a
lot older, I dressed up as a Fairy
Godmother. I told stories to
children who came into a Fairy
Shop for birthday parties. I had
wings, a wand, a sparkly dress and
cloak. We had lots of fun, but
sometimes things went wrong...
That's how I got some of my ideas
to write this story.

From Beth Norling

I tried to make fairy wings for my two-year-old daughter, but made them so heavy that they looked more like wings for a moth! When Juno wore them, they hung down her back in a very sad droopy way.

As kids we had theme parties. I would always request a "fairy party" or "ballet party." My sister had more interesting themes— one of the most bizarre was a "nose" party, with false noses and a "nose" cake!